Frog is a Hero

Max Velthuijs

Andersen Press

This paperback edition first published in 2014 by Andersen Press Ltd.
20 Vauxhall Bridge Road, London SW1V 2SA.
First published in Great Britain in 1995 by Andersen Press Ltd.
Published in Australia by Random House Australia Pty.,
20 Alfred Street, Milsons Point, Sydney, NSW 2061.

Colour separated in Switzerland by Photolitho AG, Zürich.
Printed and bound in China by Foshan Zhaorong Printing Co., Ltd.

10 9 8 7 6 5 4 3 2 1

British Library Cataloguing in Publication Data available.
ISBN 978 1 78344 144 0

Dark clouds were gathering in the sky. The sun disappeared behind the clouds.

“It’s starting to rain,” thought Frog happily. The first drops were already falling on his bare skin. Frog loved the rain.

He danced for joy as the raindrops fell thick and fast. "It's raining, it's raining. My shorts are soaking wet!" he sang loudly.

The sky got darker and darker. Now it was raining cats and dogs. This was a bit too much even for Frog. He ran home dripping wet.

Frog made himself a nice hot cup of tea. The raindrops pattered against the window but it was cosy inside.

After three days of rain however, Frog began to feel restless. He wondered how Duck and Pig and Hare were. He hadn't seen them since the rain started.

On the fifth day, the river began to rise. It wasn't long before water came streaming into Frog's house. At first, Frog thought it was funny but then he began to worry.

He hurried over to Duck's house. It was flooded there as well.
"Where is all this water coming from?" asked Duck desperately.
"The river has burst its banks," shouted Frog. "Let's go to Pig's house."

Together they waded through the watery landscape.

Pig was leaning out of her attic window.
"All my things are wet," she cried.

It was true. Tables and chairs were floating around the room. Everything was in a mess. They couldn't stay there.

"Let's go and see Hare," suggested Frog.

Hare's house was on an island in the middle of the water. Hare stood at the door and waved to them. "Come inside," he shouted. "It's dry in here."

It was warm inside. Gratefully, they dried themselves in front of the stove and told Hare how their houses had been flooded.

"You must all stay here," said Hare. "There's plenty of room and I've got plenty of food."

So they all sat down to a big pot of stew Hare had made. They were very hungry and they ate everything up. Then they settled down to a cosy evening, with the rain still pattering against the windowpanes.

They stayed as Hare's guests for days. They were happy together, while outside it rained and rained.

Then, one day, they found they were down to their last loaf of bread.

"We have no more food left," declared Hare gravely.

"We'll die if we don't get help," said Duck.

"I don't want to die," said Frog, "ever."

The next day only the last crumbs of bread were left. They were all terribly hungry, but nobody knew what to do. Outside, it had stopped raining but the water was still very high.

“I know!” shouted Frog suddenly. “I’ll swim across to those hills and fetch help.”
Hare looked concerned. “The current is very strong and it’s such a long way,” he said. “It’s too dangerous.”
“But I can manage it,” cried Frog enthusiastically. “I’m the best swimmer of us all.” They knew this was true.

So Frog stepped bravely into the water. His friends watched nervously. Soon, he disappeared into the distance.

The water was ice cold, but Frog didn't think about it. He thought of Duck and Hare and Pig who were hungry.

The further Frog swam, the stronger the current became. Frog felt tired. He was hardly making any headway. Suddenly the current carried him away.

Frog began to sink.
"I'm just a frog that can't swim any more," thought Frog. "I'll drown. I'm going to die and I'll never see my friends again."

Just then a familiar voice said, “Hello! What have we here?” Two strong arms pulled Frog out of the water and into a boat. It was Rat.

Frog told Rat all about the rain, the flood and the hunger, and how he had set out to get help.
“Don’t worry,” said Rat. “My boat is full of provisions for my travels. There’s plenty of food here for everyone.”
And he set sail for Hare’s house, where the three friends were waiting for help to arrive.

Pig, Duck and Hare cheered when they saw Frog return in a boat. But who was that with him?

Of course, it was their good friend Rat! They could hardly believe their eyes.

And Rat had so much food on board – bread, honey, jam, peanut-butter, vegetables, potatoes and much more besides.

"Rat, you've saved us," said Hare.
"No," said Rat, "you have Frog to thank for that. It was Frog who swam through the treacherous flood, risking his life to reach me."
They all looked at Frog. He was glowing with pride. It wasn't *exactly* true, but still...

From then on things got better. The friends celebrated their rescue, and Frog was the hero. The sun was shining again and the water was beginning to go down.

After a couple of days, the water had gone. Frog, Duck and Pig were able to return to their homes.

But everything was dirty and muddy.
"No problem," said Rat, and with his help, they fixed things up just as they had been before.
But things weren't quite the same as before. None of them would ever forget the terrible flood.